SIMONE SAYS HANDS IN THE AIR

A SHORT STORY

ALEXANDRIA BLAELOCK

BlueMere Books
MELBOURNE, AUSTRALIA

For permission requests, please contact
enquiries@bluemerebooks.com.

Ordering Information:
Discounts are available on quantity purchases. For details, contact orders@bluemerebooks.com.

Simone Says Hands in the Air/Alexandria Blaelock
paperback ISBN: 978-1-925749-14-4
digital ISBN: 978-1-925749-15-1

Book Layout © BookDesignTemplates.com

BlueMere Books
www.bluemerebooks.com

SIMONE SAYS HANDS IN THE AIR

They say you should live each day as if it's your last. Follow your dreams, take risks, die empty. All that junk.

I can't say that was top of mind on the last day of my life. But as I fell, looking up at the radiant face of the woman I love, I couldn't help thinking that in so far as last days go, it had been a pretty good one.

Even knowing the end, I can't say I'd change a single detail. Except maybe, given I wouldn't face the consequences, eating something really spicy for lunch.

It started off ordinarily enough.

The same stupid radio announcer making the same stupid jokes. The snooze button giving me almost enough time to go back to sleep. The news report six minutes late instead of five.

The same coffee, the same breakfast of poached egg with ham on toast.

I nicked the dimple in my chin while shaving and grunted manfully as my cologne stung the cut. The hot water in the shower seemed to take forever to warm up.

I ran out of deodorant and didn't have a spare can.

Dressed in the same charcoal polywool suit, same stripy "trust me" corporate tie, same style of white shirt, same black shoes and socks.

All more or less the same as usual. Nothing to suggest the day would end so differently to all the ones that came before.

The traffic was unusually bad, a truck had crashed on the freeway, losing its load and closing down half the lanes.

I texted Mr Norris, my boss, I'd be late then tried not to stress. I focused on repeating the positive affirmations from my self-help audio book.

"I am ready for whatever today brings."

"I possess the strength to deal with this."

"I am unstoppable."

But things like that always unsettle you, no matter how much you'd like to think they don't.

And walking, shoulders hunched, across the Gothic style banking chamber to my station, I was conscious of the eyes of my colleagues following my progress.

We were all preparing for Mr Norris's inevitable explosion of rage. He was so angry all the time, it's a wonder he hadn't died of an apoplectic heart attack years before.

And that's about where my day started going off the rails.

Before Mr Norris had even stood up and drawn breath to start screaming, three men in blue boiler suits and yellow high visibility vests burst through the door shouting.

As if that wasn't bad enough, they were wearing those expensive semi-transparent latex masks, the ones you can see through.

They weren't superheroes or American presidents, they were animals which was somehow more upsetting than people would have been.

Oh, and they were waving scary-looking shotguns about too.

A Wolf stood by the door to prevent escape, a Rabbit and a Sheep took up positions to either side of the counter, effectively hemming those of us in the chamber in.

They waved their guns shouting things like "Freeze - don't move," and "Stop, or I'll shoot," or "Don't move or I'll kill you."

Obviously, the customers screamed and fled in all directions, but the robbers caught them as they ran and herded them to the centre of the highly polished, ornately tiled marble floor.

Another two robbers in the same clothing slipped in during the confusion. A Tabby Cat locked the door before taking the fourth corner, while a Tiger leapt on the counter and shot at the ceiling.

"Get your phones out and hand 'em over," he shouted.

I couldn't help flinching.

Not because I was scared, or startled by the noise, the fear hadn't kicked in at that point, but because of the destruction of the beautiful heritage-listed plasterwork.

I'd spent hours gazing up at it, pretending to think. I thought I'd never be able to look at it again without remembering this incident.

Wolf and Tabby Cat pulled bags from their pockets and started collecting the phones. After he'd taken mine, Wolf threw me onto the squirming heap of customers/hostages, in the centre of the chamber.

Rabbit calmly walked along the counter and leaned over to place the muzzle of his shotgun against Simone's forehead. He shouted "Where's the manager? If you don't come out now, I'm going to kill her."

Poor beautiful Simone, with her big blue eyes and long blond hair.

In her uniform, she looked and acted like the epitome of hard, soulless banking efficiency, but

I knew she had the heart of a marshmallow inside.

Soft and warm - fluffy and sticky if she liked you but hard and repellent if she didn't.

To be honest, I was surprised no one had activated the security barriers, but it looked to be too late now.

I struggled to get off the floor to help Simone, but Tabby Cat hit me in the chest with the butt of his shotgun, and I fell back.

Simone cried out and started to reach out towards me, but Rabbit pushed his shotgun more firmly against her head, and she stood down.

"I mean it, I'll kill her."

Mr Norris, the weasel, stayed quiet and still for the first time in living memory.

One of our less than happy customers was incensed and all but stood up, pointing and shouting "he's over there."

A couple of the tellers, terrified as they were, smiled grimly.

I think one of the robbers may have snorted.

I don't mind admitting I was thoroughly satisfied and resolved to give that customer anything he wanted the next time he asked.

Rabbit allowed his shotgun to fall, hanging from the sling around his shoulders and Simone slumped with relief. He walked across the chamber, shotgun barrel knocking against his leg, to Mr Norris who was trying to scoot backwards away.

Like a child, sliding across the floor.

Rabbit scowled, and demonstrating little respect for Mr Norris's seniority, and pulled him off the floor by his tie.

Also very satisfying.

You can call me petty, but I hope Mr Norris regrets his cowardice for the rest of a very long life. He probably won't, he's not the kind of person who thinks deeply or takes serious moral reflection, but I hope there is such a thing as karma.

Though I wonder a little if the day might have turned out differently if he'd been a better man.

Ah well, too late now.

Anyway, Rabbit hauled the choking Mr Norris back across the room and slammed him up against the cage's security door, "open it."

Mr Norris started bleating some nonsense or other, so Rabbit smacked him up against the door again.

You might wonder at this point why still no one behind the counter had activated the security barrier, but I can't help thinking they just wanted to see Mr Norris suffer.

It's quite possible they were afraid and not thinking clearly, but he was deeply disliked by all of us.

If you "manage" people, you might like to remember that one day your life might literally be in their hands.

Mr Norris gave in and pulled the keys from his pocket. Rabbit snatched them from his hand, pushing him to the floor. Weirdly, he let Mr Norris scuttle unharmed back to the "safety" of the hostage huddle.

As Rabbit put the key in the door, Tiger jumped down from the counter and met him there, "right, you lot, get out here."

As the tellers started filing out of the cage, Simone bringing up the rear, Tabby pulled me to my feet and towards the staff door.

Even though it seemed he was treating me more respectfully than Mr Norris, I was starting to feel afraid.

But I felt a duty to keep my colleagues and customers safe, "I possess the strength to deal with this," I quietly told myself.

"I am ready for whatever today brings."

Tabby said nothing, perhaps he didn't hear.

Tiger pointed the tellers toward the other hostages, but as Simone was about to leave the cage, Rabbit caught her arm and held her back.

Tabby pushed me through the door and closed it, locking everyone else out.

I looked at Simone, she seemed okay given she'd just had a gun pointed at her head.

Maybe she'd gone through the fear barrier and come out calm and collected, but a little bit psychotic on the other side.

Rabbit waved his shotgun in the direction of the strongroom, and I pushed Simone ahead of me in case she did something stupid.

Or Rabbit did.

"I possess the strength to deal with this," I thought to myself.

The strongroom looks like a cross between a prison for cupboards and a bus station locker room.

The prison bit is for bank storage, and the locker bit for customer safety deposit boxes.

Customers can't get into the bank section, but bank staff can access the lockboxes through the bank bit.

Which at that moment seemed like it might not be the best arrangement.

Rabbit gave Simone the keys, "unlock it," he said. She sorted through the bunch, found the right one, inserted it into the lock and turned it.

I thought she'd push the door open, but she let go of the key and stood back allowing him to open the gate and take the keys.

He pulled a bag from his pocket, "you two, in there and fill the bag." Simone took the bag and dragged me in behind her.

Rabbit pulled the door closed behind us, and we watched as he opened the gate to the safety deposit section and disappeared from view.

Simone let out a ragged sob and leaned into my chest.

I tucked her head under my chin and folded her into my arms. We stood still for a moment while I enjoyed the warmth of her body against mine and the fresh herbal scent of her hair.

I wish we could have spent eternity in that moment, but all too soon she said, "he'll be back any second, we'd better fill this bag before he gets here."

Reluctantly I kissed the top of her head and let her go.

"It'll be okay," I said, "we'll get through this."

She smiled faintly and opened the cash cupboard.

"I'll hold the bag, and you stuff it," she said.

Our cash stocks had been replenished more than usual for a couple of salary payments the day before, so there was a lot of money in there.

I found myself wondering whether it would all fit in the bag.

Not that I was worried or anything, it was just a sort of puzzle to take the edge of the tension.

Though I wondered what Rabbit might do if there was too much left in the cupboard.

"I am ready for whatever today brings," I thought to myself.

It seemed longer, but by the time Rabbit came back, about five minutes later, we'd managed to cram about 80% of the cash into the bag.

He let us out of the strongroom and said, "thank you," as Simone handed him the bag.

He clipped it onto a carabiner attached to his shotgun strap and gestured for us to proceed him back to the main banking chamber.

I don't know how the police found out, but as we passed through the security door, I heard the sirens.

Rabbit cocked his head to listen and gestured at Tiger who did the same. The other three drew closer into a protective circle around the hostages.

Tiger and Rabbit held a heated, whispered conversation in front of the open security door.

I couldn't hear exactly what they said, but there was a lot of gesturing with the guns.

If it was me, I'd be arguing about how to get out without being captured.

Maybe Tiger wanted to shoot some hostages.

I took Simone's hand and started sidling away, but Rabbit noticed and grabbed her other arm.

"How do we get out without using the front door, or attracting any attention?" he whispered.

She opened her mouth a couple of times, but couldn't speak, so I said, "if you take the back stairs up a couple of flights, you can access the building next door and might be able to get away from there."

"Show me," he said, letting go of Simone and pulling my right arm up behind my back to push me ahead of him.

Tiger took hold of Simone, and the other robbers fell in behind us.

I led the way back through the security door, and Sheep closed it behind us.

Just before we hit the strongroom, I turned towards a nondescript door, awkwardly punched my security code in the door handle and pushed it open.

I had a half-formed idea that somehow I could get hold of Simone and shut the robbers out, but Rabbit seemed determined to take me with them.

He pushed me out in front of him, like a shield, and satisfied that the stairwell was at that moment secure, told the others "it's safe."

In the mad scramble up the stairs, I didn't notice I was the only one being held.

Somewhere in the ascent, marshmallow Simone was replaced by someone harder and crueller. Someone more scheming criminal and less hapless victim.

Someone as scary as those shotguns. Maybe even more.

The bridge between the buildings was on the fourth floor. It was open to the elements, and on occasion, you'd see smokers sneaking a quick ciggie between the pot plants even though it was a smoke-free area.

Funny how insignificant it seemed now when just a few days prior I had been complaining about it.

As we reached the platform, Rabbit let go of my arm, and keeping an eye on us, gestured for the robbers to check the area.

With it secured, they gathered around so they could talk.

I turned back to check on Simone, "are you hurt? Are you okay?"

She laughed.

Not her usual modestly gentle laugh, but one that was hard and hysterical.

It went on and on, she bent over, tears streaming down her face but unable to stop.

I was just thinking I should probably slap her, when she spluttered to a gasping stop, breathing heavily with the odd snort leaking through.

"When I heard the police siren I was terrified we wouldn't make it for a minute there. I thought we were done for."

"We still might not make it." I gestured at the robbers. "what do you think they're planning?"

"Hopefully, how we can get away without being caught."

"Surely they'll tie us up or something and leave us here when they go?"

Beautiful Simone looked up at me and gently placed her hand against my cheek.

"You still don't get it, do you? This was my heist - I planned it. They are my guys."

My mouth fell open.

My meek and mild Simone?

I was surprised to say the least.

On the one hand, I was impressed by her audaciousness, but on the other, horrified that she was not the law-abiding citizen I'd assumed she was.

I mean you don't, do you?

You just assume the people you know and love and eat lunch with are just like you. It never occurred to me to think of her as a scheming criminal who knew no limits.

I shut my mouth as I realised that the only way I was going to escape was to join her gang.

Now I knew she was a criminal kingpin, it didn't seem likely she'd let me go alive.

She was looking at me closely, and I knew I should say something to reassure her.

But what do you say when your girlfriend turns out to be a criminal mastermind responsible for what will be the last, worst morning of your life.

Positive self-help affirmations don't really prepare you for that.

"Um, no."

She smiled at the shock on my face, and I tried to be comforted, but it was the alligator smile of a crazy person.

The kid of crazy person who'd push you in front of a bus as a joke.

I stepped back involuntarily, but of course, it was the wrong thing to do. It made her angry.

"Don't you think I'm clever?"

"Um, yes. But why rob your own bank?"

She laughed again, the kind of cruel laugh you hear on TV prank shows.

"It's not about the money darling, it's about what's on the thumb drive we retrieved from a deposit box."

I couldn't quite grasp that, "oh. Are you a spy then?"

"You are the most innocent creature, so adorable, " she said. "I know that's why I chose you, but you surprise me every time."

I guess that meant that she liked me too, did that mean the affirmations were working?

Not that it mattered, right then I thought she was as appealing as a bucket of cold sick.

A really big bucket.

I wasn't at all happy about her revelation, but when you're in love, you do dumb things.

"Let's get away from here, I won't tell anyone. We can hide in a country town somewhere. No one needs to know about this."

Not the right thing to say.

"Charlie, I don't want to run away and hide. I want everyone to know what I've done. And if I trigger the biggest manhunt in history, that's so much the better. Don't you want to be Bonnie to my Clyde?"

"I might be wrong, but I don't think their romance ended well."

She laughed again. "Charlie, don't you want to die in a blaze of glory?"

I really didn't.

"I was leaning more towards old age in my comfortable bed. Grieving wife and children by my side."

"Poor Charlie. You're going to die anyway." And she pushed me playfully.

But what neither of us had noticed was how close we were to the edge of the bridge.

Her nudge was enough to leave me teetering on the edge of the handrail.

And when I lost my balance, I fell backwards, arms flailing from the bridge.

All in all, it was over almost before my terror mounted.

My last sight was Simone's beautiful face, alive with elation, and I'd like to think a little despair.

THE END

ABOUT THE AUTHOR

Alexandria Blaelock writes stories, some of them for *Ellery Queen's Mystery Magazine* and *Pulphouse Fiction Magazine*. She's also written four self-help books applying business techniques to personal matters like getting dressed, cleaning house, and feeding your friends.

As a recovering Project Manager, she's probably too fond of sticking to plan. She lives in a forest because she enjoys birdsong, the scent of gum leaves and the sun on her face. When not telecommuting to parallel universes from her Melbourne based imagination, she watches K-dramas, talks to animals, and drinks Campari. At the same time.

Discover more at www.alexandriablaelock.com.

OTHER SHORT STORIES BY ALEXANDRIA BLAELOCK

Kiss of Death
Long Weekend in the Snow
Shining Star
Phoenix Child
Ship in a Bottle
Lady of the Looking Glass
Simone Says Hands in the Air
Life in the Security Directorate
Fate in Your Hands
Love in the Security Directorate
Alma's Grace
Payton's Run
The Guardian's Vigil
The Life and Death of Carmelita Basingstoke
Balancing the Book

BOOKS BY ALEXANDRIA BLAELOCK

Stress Free Dinner Parties
Build Your Signature Wardrobe
Holistic Personal Finance
Ms Blaelock's Book of Minimally Viable
Housekeeping